Mystery of the Skinny Sophomore

The Dallas O'Neil Mysteries

MYSTERY OF THE SKINNY SOPHOMORE

by

JERRY B. JENKINS

MOODY PRESS
CHICAGO

This Guideposts edition is published by special
arrangement with Moody Press

ISBN: 0-8024-8387-9

4 5 6 Printing/LC/Year 93 92 91

Printed in the United States of America

To the Barnes brothers—
Bruce, Jim, and Dennis

Contents

1. Traci Kent   9

2. Staying Alive   17

3. Extra Innings   25

4. Down to the Wire   33

5. The Big Finish   41

6. Fat?!   49

7. The Semifinals   57

8. The Tryouts   65

9. The Problem   73

10. The Finals   81

11. The Referral   89

1

Traci Kent

Andy Kent had a sister who was a knockout. Traci was a sophomore with long, bouncy, dark hair. She had been a cheerleader at our elementary school from fourth through sixth grade, then all through junior high and as a high school freshman.

My best friend, Jimmy Calabresi, and I, not to mention just about everybody else in the Baker Street Sports Club, had major problems with Andy. But we thought his sister was something. Fun to be around, fun to talk to, fun to look at. She was very athletic, and she was pretty.

The problem with her little brother was that he was not honest. There's no gentle way to say it. I admit I was at fault in much of my trouble with Andy. As president of the sports club and captain of the baseball team, it was my job to choose the starters, position the players, and set the batting order. Andy was the best fielder of the last three players on the team, and he was about equal to the other two in hitting. So, he played right field and batted ninth.

Nobody is thrilled with that, but somebody has to do it. I thought he would be glad to be in the starting line-up at all, but he thought he should be the lead-off hitter. I told him he didn't make enough contact with the ball or get on base often enough, and he said it was because he didn't get up to bat often enough.

He also complained about being left out of batting practice too often, and he was right. I forgot to have BP in reverse order as I had promised. A couple of times in a row we ran out of time, or it was too hot, and he didn't get in his batting practice.

I didn't realize how insensitive I had been to him, but he never said much either. He was mad at me for not thinking he was better, mad at Jimmy because Jimmy's new horse captured everybody's attention, and mad at Matt for hitting ahead of him in the line-up, even as a reserve.

That was why he sneaked out one night and turned Jimmy's horse loose, making tracks in the corral while wearing first my baseball shoes, then Matt's. The horse was found, and Andy eventually confessed, but then the real work began. I wanted to prove to Andy that if he was really sorry, he could make it up to us by being a good club member and teammate.

By the start of the school year in the fall, when we were in the last week of our post-season baseball tournament, Andy had done fairly well. He confessed to the whole team, asked us to forgive him and give him another chance, apologized to Jimmy and Matt and me, and was pretty quiet the rest of the season.

His sister came to a lot of the games, which made us even more eager to be nice to him and keep him in the club. She really knew sports. Sometimes, just for fun, she and her cheerleader-type friends would make up cheers and jump around, shouting them while we played. Nobody ever cheered along with them, and they usually ended up in laughter, but it was fun to have them there anyway.

The girls practiced and practiced for cheerleader tryouts. They were scheduled for next Friday and would be just in time for the start of the high school football season. Even though nobody in the Baker Street Sports Club was even in junior high yet, a lot of their big brothers and sisters were in high school. We all went to most of the varsity games.

Andy's sister, Traci, was the favorite to become captain of the varsity cheerleading squad, even though she was only a sophomore.

"It's her personality," her brother bragged. "Everybody loves her except us."

"Us?" I said. "Who's us?"

"Her family."

"You love her," I said. "You're her brother."

"Yuck!" Andy said.

"Well, you're not supposed to *like* your sister. Nobody *likes* his sister. But you love her, and surely your parents do."

"What they love is how smart and popular and successful she is."

"That's nice," I said. "I'm sure they're proud of her."

Andy shook his head. "That's not what I call it. I wouldn't want to live with that kind of pressure."

"What kind?"

"Can't even get a B on her report card. I wouldn't mind havin' one."

"Maybe your parents don't expect as much from you."

" 'Course they don't, and that's just the way I want it."

I didn't understand. "Why wouldn't you want to do well and make your parents proud of you? I do."

"Your parents would be proud of you no matter what you did, O'Neil."

"Not quite."

"Almost. If my parents thought I was able to get straight A's like my sister, I'd never hear the end of it."

"I'll bet they're excited about this cheerleader business."

"You bet."

When I saw Traci at our opening tournament game that Wednesday, I wished her luck. She didn't say thanks. She didn't smile. She just pursed her lips and nodded gravely.

"Just two days away, huh?" I said.

"Don't remind me."

"What time are tryouts?"

"After school."

"When do you find out if you're captain?"

"Monday morning."

"You'll get it," I said.

She didn't say anything. In fact, she appeared not to have even heard me, though I know she did.

That night at our game, the three girls Traci came with went through their silly cheerleading antics, but Traci sat on the bottom row of the bleachers with her chin in her hands, staring. It seemed she didn't move. Every time I looked at her she was sitting that way, her eyes locked on the pitcher. Occasionally one of her friends would come over and say something to her, but if she responded she did it without turning her head or looking at her friends.

We were in an eight-team tournament at the Park City Little League fields. It was a single-elimination set-up, the quarterfinals played Wednesday, the semifinals Thursday, and the finals Saturday. We were in the top bracket where Highland had beat Forest in the early evening opener. In the lower bracket Deerfield had edged Wheaton in extra innings. While we played Lake County on Field One under the lights, Park City would play Beach Park on Field Two. The winners would play the next night in the semifinals.

The tough part about this tournament was that each pitcher could pitch only six innings. That meant you needed at least three pitchers, and you had to decide whether you saved your strongest pitcher until the finals or used him early to insure staying in it.

We decided to try something very different. Cory would start and throw as hard as he could for two innings. Even if he had a perfect game going, he would come out for Bugsy and play second base. Bugsy would do the same on the mound for two innings, then play short, and I would pitch. We would do this in every game, making our opponents, we hoped, feel like they were facing a string of hard-throwing relief pitchers. If we went into extra innings, I had no idea what we'd do.

Before the game I read off the starting line-up to the guys. We would bat last. "Cory leading off and pitching. Bugsy at second. Me at short. Toby at third. Jack at first. Ryan in center. Brent in left. Jimmy catching. Andy in right."

Andy used to sigh loudly every time he heard that, but now he just nodded and ran out to his position.

Cory was wild and quickly grew angry with himself and the umpire in the top of the first. He walked three of the first four batters he faced, and the fourth popped out to Toby at third. Cory was stomping around the mound and smacking his glove.

I jogged in to talk to him.

"Let 'em hit, Cor'," I said. "We can't defend against walks."

"What do you want me to do—lay it right in there?"

"Yes! Give them something to hit! What's the difference if you walk them in or they drive them in? At least if they hit the ball we have a chance to get 'em out."

Cory over-reacted a little. Rather than just try to throw strikes, he slowed his pitches to a crawl and laid the next two right down the middle to their fifth hitter, a left-handed batter and pitcher. He drilled a long double between Andy and Ryan. By the time Ryan got the ball back in to Bugsy, who relayed it to me, the bases were cleared and we were down 3-0 with only one out and a runner in scoring position.

Their next hitter bunted the runner to third and was safe at first. A sacrifice fly and a pop out later, we came in to hit, trailing 4-0. My pitching rotation strategy looked foolish.

Cory was still seething as he waited to lead off the bottom of the first. "Try to bunt your way on," I told him.

"Are you kidding? I want to hit one outta here. That left field foul line is only a hundred eighty feet away."

"That's about forty feet farther than you can hit," I said. "What do you want to fly out to left for when you can get on base and score a run?"

"A run isn't gonna help us much after my wonderful first inning," he said, jamming his helmet down over his red, curly hair.

"Cory, just do what I say, OK? Bunt your way on. Their infielders are going to be playing back because this left-hander is a junk baller and throws slow."

"That's why I think I can hit one out."

Now I was mad. I thought we had a chance at reaching the finals of this tournament, and I wasn't thrilled at being down 4-0 any more than Cory was. "You want a chance to redeem yourself in the top of the second?" I asked him.

"I'd understand if you pulled me off the mound. I stink."

"You don't stink. If it hadn't been for the walks, we'd be right in this game. Going for a home run when we're down this much doesn't make sense. I want you to bunt, and if you don't, I'm pulling you out of the game completely."

He scowled and shook his head.

I watched from just inside the dugout as Bugsy waited on deck. The first pitch from the left-hander was his idea of a fastball. It was straight and waist high, a home-run pitch if there ever was one. Cory, looking fierce and determined, stepped as if to take a big swing, then held up. Strike one. The third baseman backed up a step.

Cory stared over at me as if to say he could have hit that one a mile.

"Take him downtown, Cory!" I said.

"He hittin' away?" Bugsy asked.

"Nope. Layin' one down."

"Doesn't look like it."

"That's good strategy, Bugs, don't you think? They're not expecting a bunt when we're down by four."

He shrugged. "He could have hit that first pitch out of here."

14

"I just hope he lays off the next one unless it's perfect for bunting. I don't want him to give away his plan, and this pitcher probably can't throw two strikes in a row."

I was right. The next pitch was similar to the first, but it rode in high at about the shoulders. Cory made it look as if he could hardly lay off it, but he did. One and one. Then I began to wonder. Was Cory defying me? Testing me? Was he planning to hit away as soon as he got his pitch?

The other manager hollered to his pitcher, "Marty, keep it down! Good hitter!"

Was he guessing, or did he know? I didn't think these teams had scouted us, but if they did, they would know Cory almost always got wood on the ball.

I turned to look up and down the bench to be sure everybody's heads and eyes were in the game. They were, except for Andy's. He sat in the far corner of the dugout, looking back at his sister in the front row.

He looked worried. She just sat and stared.

I turned back to the game just in time to see Cory leap from his normal batting stance to lay a bunt down the left side between the pitcher and third base. The startled third baseman charged across in front of the short stop, got tangled with the pitcher, then grabbed the ball and threw it over the first baseman's head. Cory wound up at second, grinning.

"Do the same thing, Bugs," I said.

"Same side?" he asked.

"No, the other side. They're not gonna expect the first three hitters to bunt."

"You're gonna bunt too?"

"No matter what happens to you," I said. We needed to peck away at that lead.

2

Staying Alive

Bugsy's bunt was not so well-placed as Cory's, but it was every bit as successful. He tried to push it up the first base line, but the Lake County pitcher had tried a sidearm sweep motion that brought his slow curve from the outside in on a right-handed hitter. The ball rode in on Bugsy, and he bunted it right back to the mound.

Bugsy took off for first in that flying motion of his, but he would have been out easily had the pitcher merely fielded the ball and tossed it over there. Cory could see what was happening and knew he would be at least sacrificed over, so he screamed and hollered as he ran, then fell down on purpose about ten feet from the bag at third.

The pitcher looked as if he were going to try to throw the ball before he caught it, then composed himself and cleanly fielded it. Bugsy wasn't even half way to first yet, so the pitcher glanced at Cory, noticed him struggling on the ground, and decided to throw to third instead. Being left-handed, all he had to do was sweep his arm across his body.

That was just what Cory wanted. As soon as he saw the pitcher straighten up to throw, he scrambled to his feet and dived into third, safe. We had runners at first and third and nobody out.

Bugsy knew I was going to bunt; Cory didn't. I knew it was the last thing Lake County would dream of. Our regular season statistics had appeared in the newspaper, so Lake County knew that three of us had been in double figures in home runs. Ryan had fifteen, Toby eleven, and I had ten.

I was all the way down on the end of the bat and trying to give every hint that I was swinging away. The first thing I wanted to do was to give Bugsy a chance to steal second. He's fast enough that he doesn't have to wait for a signal. He can go whenever he thinks he can make it. And with a runner at third and no one out, we didn't expect a play at second. Most teams fake the throw to second, and the catcher fires to the pitcher or the shortstop, who cuts off the throw and tries to get the runner at home.

That's exactly what happened on the first pitch. Bugsy broke for second, Cory danced off third, the catcher threw, the shortstop cut off the ball, but Cory stayed at third. Now my bunt was even more important. If Cory was alert, he could score, but if I surprised him, he could get caught in a rundown.

I was over-eager on the first pitch and tried to get my bat on a ball that kept rising out of the strike zone. I missed it, but it tipped off Lake County that I might bunt. The first and third basemen moved in a few steps. I still wanted to try. I didn't want to bunt to third because the third baseman would have the play at home right in front of him, not to mention Bugsy coming from second if he thought he could make it.

If I pushed it up the first base line and could get by the first baseman, maybe we'd be safe all around. I tried but fouled the ball off. Now I was down oh and two, and I couldn't afford to try to bunt again. For some reason, Marty already looked tired on the mound. He had a big lead, and though he was in a jam we still hadn't scored. He should have been confident he could hold us to just one or two runs. But his next three pitches were all inside and high, and it was all I could do to lay off them.

I should have been content with a walk, loading the bases for Toby, then Jack, then Ryan. But I was too eager to drive in a run or two. The next pitch came in high and inside again but not so far out of the strike zone that I couldn't reach it. Had I taken it, it would have been ball four, but I thought I could drive it, so I swung hard. I knew it was a mistake as soon as I started, but I was committed, so I tried to get as much of the ball as I could.

I sent a towering foul ball down the third base line. It had a lot of spin and began curving toward the metal fence about twenty feet past the bag and deep in foul territory. There was no way the ball was going to drop in fair, so even though I had started toward first, I just stopped and hung onto my bat, watching the flight of the ball and hoping it would drop over the fence, out of play.

The Lake County third baseman had been close to the bag and was late getting started after the ball. Their shortstop had the best angle on it, and he was off in a flash, eyes on the ball, scampering toward the fence. He was going full tilt when the third baseman shouted, "Look out!" The shortstop glanced down to see he was about to run into the fence, skidded to a stop, looked back up, saw the ball dropping over the fence, leaped, reached, and snagged it in the web of his glove as he fell.

What happened next made me as proud of my team as I've ever been. Both Cory and Bugsy had known to get back to their bases and tag up. As soon as that ball was caught, both took off. The third baseman was congratulating the shortstop and helping him up when they heard their teammates screaming to throw the ball home.

Cory had already scored easily, without even sliding. Kyle, coaching third, waved Bugsy around. That was a gutsy, risky play, but the shortstop was so proud of his difficult catch and so confused about runners advancing on a foul ball that he first looked at the third baseman, and then threw late. Bugsy was safe too.

I had swung at a bad pitch with two strikes and been credited with no time at bat, a sacrifice fly, and two runs batted in.

While the Lake County coach argued that runners can't advance on a foul ball—and the umpire assured him they could, advising him that in the future his third baseman should think about letting that ball drop harmlessly foul rather than catching it in a spot where he didn't have a good throw to the plate—I called our team around.

"That was the most heads-up we've been all year," I said. "Cory, Bugsy, Kyle, great job! I know we can win this game now. This guy's so slow you'll want to switch to heavier bats. Let's get 'em!"

After Toby flied out to deep left, Jack lined out to the shortstop on the hardest hit ball of the inning.

As we took the field, we heard cheering from the other diamond and saw the bright green uniforms of the Beach Bearcats circling the bases. The scoreboard showed them leading the host Park City all-stars 6-0 in the top of the second inning. If they won, they would play Deerfield the next night.

Second base was an unusual position for me, because I usually played short or pitched. As I scanned the field to get my bearings and position myself properly, I noticed that Andy was not in right field yet.

"Yo! Ryan!" I shouted. "Where's Andy?"

He shrugged, then pointed to the dugout.

I whirled around to see Andy standing with his back to the field, talking with his sister. "Kent!" I hollered. "You playin' or talkin'? Get out here!"

Andy turned and scowled at me, then turned back to his sister.

"Kyle!" I called. "You're in right for Andy! Check in with the umpire."

That brought Andy spinning out of the dugout. "Forget it! I'm here!" he said.

As he ran past me I stopped him. "Andy, you know we all run onto the field together. We can't have you talking to the fans during the game. You've been doing so well."

"That's was no fan, Dallas. That was my sister, and she's having a bad time."

"What does that mean?"

"She's so nervous about cheerleader tryouts Friday afternoon she's thinking about not even going."

"How can she be captain if she doesn't even try out for the squad?"

"She can't! That's what I've been trying to tell her. Will you talk to her?"

"Me? Why would she listen to me?"

"You'd be surprised."

"I'll think about it, but let's get back in this game, huh?"

Cory settled down in the second inning, and while he allowed two base runners, one on a walk and one on my throwing error, he didn't give up any runs.

I shook his hand as we left the field. "Good job, Cor'," I said. "I'll play short for Bugsy while he pitches, and you can get back to second."

"Yeah," he said, "we need somebody over there who can throw the ball." He was kidding.

I smiled. "Well, let's just hope Bugsy and I don't give up four runs each during our two innings."

Two identical, fantastic plays by the Lake County shortstop left us with two outs and nobody on in the bottom of the second. Ryan and Brent both grounded hard right up the middle, causing the shortstop to sprint past the bag at second, field the ball on the run, and fire to first. With his foul catch, Jack's hard liner to him, and the fact that he'd already walked twice and scored a run, he had proved to be a star.

Jimmy Calabresi was up, and I knew he was eager. He could have just as easily hit higher in the line-up, but taking the catching equipment off and putting it back on is always a hassle, and we usually avoid that, in the first inning at least, by

21

having him bat eighth. He doesn't mind, and he gives us some punch at that end of the line-up.

We had not fooled Lake County by putting Jimmy eighth. They knew he was a good hitter, and their coaches kept hollering out to the mound, "Keep it low and outside, Marty! Low and outside!"

Jimmy has a pretty good technique for adjusting to low pitching. He strides farther, and that allows him more leverage on a low swing. I tried it a few times and found myself off balance and not able to swing as hard, but somehow Jimmy makes it work.

Marty threw two balls low and outside, then caught the corner at the knee for a one and two count. I was in the third base coaching box, and Jimmy looked at me as if to say, "If he throws that one again, I'm teeing off."

I flashed him the bunt sign, and his eyes grew wide. He stepped out of the box and moved toward me.

I doubled over and laughed. "Just kidding!" I said. I'm sure I was gonna have a hitter like Jimmy—a runner as slow as Jimmy—bunt with two strikes and two outs when we were down by two in the bottom of the second.

"Hit away, big guy," I said.

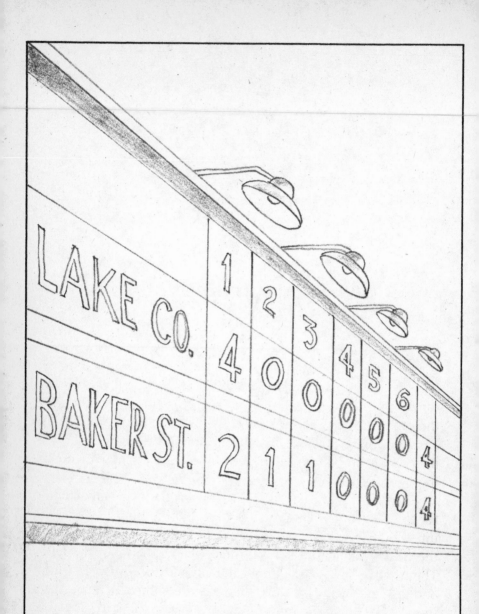

3

Extra Innings

None of us knew Lake County's lefty starter had a screw-ball, a curve that breaks away from a right-handed hitter. It sure surprised Jimmy. He thought the next pitch was identical to the last. It was spinning, but appeared to be heading for the outside corner at the knees. Jimmy overstrode and swung hard, but the ball broke away from him at the last instant. He just got the end of the bat on the ball and sent a high arc down the right field line.

It was so high that the first and second basemen actually turned and started running for it. So did the right fielder. The infielders slowed and stopped when they were half way out there and realized the ball was much deeper than they thought. The right fielder jogged under the skying ball, drifting farther and farther toward the foul line. And the home run fence. The umpire ran down the right field line too, watching to see if the ball would land fair.

It did. About two feet past the fence, where the outfielder couldn't get a glove on it. It was the highest, slowest, laziest home run I had ever seen. I was jumping when Jimmy rounded third, and I clapped him on the back.

"What a guy has to do to get his best friend's attention," he said. And he wasn't smiling. I guess I had been ignoring him. I'd talk to him about it when it was my turn to pitch.

Andy struck out and walked directly to his position. Cory tossed him his glove as he moved out toward second, and I heard him say, "I didn't know anybody could strike out against somebody as slow as Marty, but I must've forgot about you."

Andy swore at Cory.

"Same to you!" Cory said.

"Hey!" I said, jogging over. "Knock it off, you guys. We're only down by one here, so let's stay in the game."

"Did you hear what he said to me?" Cory demanded.

"I heard. I also heard what you said to him. What do you expect?"

"I expect him to be able to hit a candy pitcher like this."

"Andy, get out to right," I said. "Cory, c'mere."

He sighed and came closer.

"What's the point?" I asked. "You expect him to hit better after you belittle him? He has enough trouble getting the bat on the ball. You say something like that to him, he shoots back the only way he knows how, then you get offended. What kind of a teammate are you?"

In the past, Cory would have reacted angrily to me, but he was taking this.

"And when I asked you what you expected, I wasn't talking about what you expected in his hitting. I was talking about what you expected him to say when you're so mean to him. We have to play together as a team if we want to win this tournament."

"Let's go, boys," the umpire said. "Play ball."

"What do you want me to do, Dallas?"

"Encourage him. You'll probably give him a heart attack."

Cory jogged to second, his head down. When he turned to look behind him at Andy in right, Andy was staring at him. Cory gave him a thumbs up sign, a sort of combination apology and encouragement.

Andy waved at him self-consciously.

Something caught my eye near the stands behind our dug-out. I don't know why or how I noticed, but something—some-one—was missing. Traci Kent. When had she left? Where did she go? Had she come only to watch Andy hit? Where was I supposed to talk to her later, if Andy still wanted me to? I looked out to him, but he either hadn't noticed she was gone or didn't care. I couldn't worry about it then.

Bugsy had a little trouble finding the plate with his pitches, and if it hadn't been for over-eagerness on the part of Lake County hitters, he might have walked the bases loaded, just as Cory had. Bugsy fell behind in the count on every hitter, but he got the first to pop out to Jack at first base, saw the next reach on a dropped third strike—Jimmy was really mad at himself—and found himself down two and oh on the next.

I knew Bugsy liked to slow his pitches when he got behind on hitters, so I hollered over to Cory to cover second on a steal, and I shaded more toward third. If the hitter pulled one of Bugsy's slower pitches, I'd be in better position to field it, but I would be too far from second to take the throw on a steal at-tempt.

Bugsy crossed me up. He must have noticed the runner breaking for second because he hurried his pitch and threw it fairly fast. It rode in on the wrists of the hitter, who fought it off and looped a low liner right to the bag at second. Cory, who had drifted over as the runner broke, straddled second and caught the ball on the first base side of the bag, as if it had been thrown.

The runner, a speedy infielder, had gotten a good jump and probably would have beaten a throw, but his headfirst slide carried him right into the tag. It was about as fast a double play as I've ever seen.

Cory was thrilled. "I hate to admit it," he said, "but I wasn't even thinking double play when I tagged him. I just did that by instinct."

Cory, Bugsy, and I stood watching Marty warm up for Lake County. "I think they're trying to squeeze a game out of their worst pitcher," Bugsy said. "Surely they've got somebody better than this."

"We're still behind," I said.

"Yeah, but once we get our timing down, we'll knock this guy outta here. Our problem is we face you in practice and then we can't adjust to this slow junk."

"What do you think, boys?" I said. "Wanna bunt the day-lights out of these guys again and see if we can tie this thing up?"

"Nah," Cory said, "I feel like hittin'. Let me blast one off this guy."

"OK, but don't go for the fence. Just drive it somewhere with—"

"Yeah, I know, O'Neil, I know. Drive it somewhere with a purpose. Have an idea."

"All right, so what's your idea?"

"I'm gonna go with the pitch."

"I'll bet he jams you," Bugsy said.

"Then I'll drive it to left—with a purpose."

"And if you get on, I'm bunting again," Bugsy said. "Remember, Cory, no matter where you are, I'm bunting."

Cory nodded and looked at me. "Even on two strikes?"

"Why not?" I said. "Bugs is a good bunter. We want you in scoring position so I can knock you in. These six-inning games don't leave much room for scoring opportunities. We've got to at least tie this thing up so we've got something to work with. Let's give Bugsy a clean slate for the top of the fourth, at least."

"I wouldn't mind pitching with a lead," Bugsy said.

"I'm sure you wouldn't," I said.

"I mean," he added, "don't hold back and settle for a tie."

As if we would have if he hadn't reminded us. "Thanks, Bugs," I said solemnly. "I'll tell the other guys not to hesitate to score runs."

He grinned, his teeth shining against his dark face.

Cory slammed a long, loud foul ball to deep left that would have been a home run, had it been fair. That just made Marty afraid of Cory, and he kept the ball mostly down and outside and walked him on four straight pitches. Cory flung his bat angrily, wishing he could have gotten a hit.

"A walk's as good as a hit," I reminded him as he trotted to first. "We need base runners."

I gave him the steal sign and told Bugsy to lay off the first pitch. In a way, it was too bad because it was a gimme pitch. I mean, it was one of those gimme-that-again pitches. Marty had been so upset at walking Cory that he just laid it in there first thing on Bugsy. Cory took off with the pitcher's first motion and stole second easily.

Now was a good time for that bunt. Even if they got Bugsy at first, Cory would be at third, a duck on the pond for me. I wouldn't mind another RBI, but mostly I wanted us to tie the game. I didn't really care who was responsible.

It was a good thing because I wasn't the one who tied the game. Bugsy squared around to bunt the next pitch, and the first and third basemen came charging in. Again I was impressed with the Lake County shortstop, who darted over to cover third as Cory left second. Bugsy missed the pitch, and the catcher came up firing. The throw was high, or Cory would have been out. It was right on the money, even on the shortstop side of the bag, but Cory just got in under it.

From the on-deck circle I flashed a bunch of meaningless signs to try to confuse Lake County. Both Bugsy and Cory knew what was coming next: a suicide squeeze bunt for the tie. The pitcher wound up instead of stretching, which was perfect for us. Cory bolted toward the plate with the pitcher's first movement, and he was committed. If Bugsy missed the pitch, the catcher could put an easy tag on Cory.

The pitch came in high, too high to bunt normally, but Bugsy had to go after it for Cory's sake. Just before Cory reached the plate, Bugsy nicked the pitch with his bat and sent a tiny pop-up out just in front of the plate. The pitcher was caught off guard and froze, and when the catcher dashed out to get the ball, he was bowled over by Cory. The pitcher finally got to the ball and had the presence of mind to throw Bugsy out at first, but the game was tied.

The Lake County coaches again argued, charging interference on Cory for getting in the catcher's way of fielding the ball. The umpire explained that the base path and the plate belong to the runner unless the catcher has the ball.

I popped out to second base, over-swinging and trying for a homer to put us ahead. Sometimes I think I'll never learn. Then Toby hit a ball to the deepest part of the field, where their center fielder caught it in front of the fence. That shot was probably twenty or thirty feet farther than Jimmy's home run, but all it was was a loud out.

We had scored in every inning, but we were still just tied. Bugsy settled down and got Lake County out in order in the top of the fourth. We loaded the bases in the fourth, fifth, and sixth without scoring, and when it was my turn to pitch in the fifth and sixth, I shut out Lake County too.

It was 4-4 going into the top of the seventh, and I didn't know who should pitch.

4

Down to the Wire

The last thing I wanted to do was to use up another inning of any of the pitchers we had used so far. If we stayed in the tournament, each of us just had four more innings to pitch. I decided on another crazy scheme I hoped would work.

"Jack" I said, "I want you to pitch until you get one out. Can you do that?"

"Sure, but what if I hit someone?"

"You won't. I'll play first, and you pitch until you get an out. Then you come back to first, and I'll play third until Toby gets an out. Then, Andy, it'll be your turn."

"Me?!" Andy said, looking as if he didn't know whether to laugh or cry. "Me?"

I nodded. "All you have to get is one out. If you fall behind in the count, any of you, just lay it in there because we have to get outs. We can't have a bunch of base runners or a bunch of runs to make up in the bottom of the inning."

Andy ran out to right field yelling at one of his sister's friends. "Jill! Jill! Find Traci and tell her I'm pitching this inning!"

Jack was incredible, so much so that I wished I could just leave him in to finish the game for us. He threw straight and hard, his pitches not moving much, but unhittable anyway. He was faster than any of the three of us who had started, and because he was so huge (he's six-four, so we had to prove his age before the tournament), the Lake County hitter kept bailing out on him. By the time he got up enough courage to stand in there and try to swing, he was behind in the count one and two, and he struck out. Jack beamed.

Then it was Toby's turn. As we watched him warm up, we knew we had Lake County intimidated. They had never seen anything like him. He threw as hard as Jack, and his pitches darted this way and that too. We knew we had a good pitcher in Toby, because I often used him in practice before we faced a fast pitcher. His trouble was that he didn't have any control.

I noticed Traci Kent coming over to our field from the other one. She stood and watched Toby warm up, then I saw her talking to one of the fans.

All of a sudden she started yelling at me, right in front of everybody. "How could you do that?" she screamed. "How could you take him out after he struck somebody out?"

I wanted to ignore her, but everything and everybody on the diamond grew quiet. What did she care? I saw her open her mouth again, so I ran over to her. "What do you want?" I said.

"How can you do that to Andy?" she demanded. "You ask him to pitch without any warning, then—"

"He's thrilled," I said.

"Then he strikes out the only hitter he faces—"

"What?"

"And you pull him out? What do you want? What do you expect?"

"Traci, listen—"

"You listen, Dallas! You think you're somebody special who can just play with people's feelings, but—"

"Traci—"

"—he's only eleven years old. Maybe you're trying to get back at him for that business with Jimmy's horse, but—"

"Traci! Listen! He hasn't pitched yet!"

"What?"

"He hasn't pitched yet. Gimme a break. We can pitch only six innings each in this tournament, so I don't want to use Bugsy or Cory or me in extra innings. Nobody else has enough experience to do more than get one out, so I'm pitching three guys this inning."

"Well, someone told me Andy was pitching, and when I came over here, there was one out and Toby was warming up. I asked that guy what the first pitcher had done, and he said he had struck out a batter and was being replaced."

"That wasn't Andy. That was Jack. Andy pitches after Toby."

"Toby pitches one out too?"

"Exactly." I waited for an apology for her outburst, but it never came.

"And what if Toby allows some runners before he gets an out, then Andy comes in with runners on and the game tied?"

I shrugged. I hadn't thought of that, but it was sure a possibility, especially with Toby on the mound.

"So he could wind up the goat of this game, couldn't he?"

"Well, if the winning run scored off him and wasn't one of Toby's runners, he'd technically get the loss, yes, but—"

"You're doing this on purpose! You want to lose, and you want it to be Andy's fault!"

I was steamed. "I certainly don't want anything to look bad for Andy. If you think I want to lose, you don't know me very well."

"I don't want to know you very well either," she said. "I don't want to know you at all."

"Play ball," the umpire said.

Traci Kent turned and walked away, heading back to her friend's car. Oh, brother.

Toby started well, then got too careful and walked two batters. They both advanced on a passed ball, and we were in deep trouble. Marty lofted a long fly ball to the opposite field in left, which Brent hauled in and fired to the infield. Lake County should have scored on that play. Both their runners, however, took off when the bat hit the ball, and both had to scramble back before getting doubled off.

I thought their coaches were going to kill them. "We could have the lead right now!" they screamed.

I called time out and asked Jimmy and Bugsy to join me on the mound. I told them of the problem with Andy's sister. "I wonder if it's worth the hassle," I said. "Maybe I should let Toby finish and take responsibility for his own base runners."

"No way! You said I was pitchin', so I'm pitchin'!" It was Andy. When I went to the mound, he had come in from right field. And why not? He knew it was his turn to pitch.

I tossed him the ball, and the others moved back to their positions. I waited to replace him in right until I saw how he did. His first two warm-up pitches were uncatchable. Why had I come up with this idea anyway?

"Relax," I told him. "You can do it. Just throw strikes and keep us close so we can win it in the bottom half."

"If I hold 'em to nothin', we don't have so much pressure in the bottom of the seventh, right?"

"Right." I was impressed that he had thought that through. "We can live with a run or two, though, and it won't be your fault. Just keep us close."

"We can live with a run or two? You gotta be kiddin'. I know it won't be my fault. It'll be yours. I didn't volunteer for this. It was your idea. All I can do is the best I can do."

His next two warm-up pitches were over Jimmy's head, and that brought Jimmy running out. "He can't even get the ball over. You'd do better to let me pitch."

"I'm following through on the plan, Jim," I said. "Give him a good target." Who was Jimmy kidding? He was one of the worst pitchers I had ever seen.

Andy finished his warm-up tosses, finally throwing nice, fat, easy pitches Jimmy could get to, and I ran into right field hollering, "Two down! Let's get 'em!"

Andy's first pitch was right down the middle but in the dirt, and it was all Jimmy could do to throw himself in front of it. The runner had come half way down the line, and Jimmy jumped up and chased him back.

Over the batter's, the catcher's, and the umpire's head. Ball two. Luckily, the ball caromed right back to Jimmy, or we would have been down by a run.

A one-hopper to Jimmy's glove. Ball three.

Almost hit the batter. Ball four. Bases loaded.

Wild pitch off the backstop, all the runners move up. We're down 5-4, and I'm getting yelled at. "How long, O'Neil? Get a pitcher in there!" Five straight pitches, not even close.

I jogged in and asked Jack to replace me in right. I should have asked Jack to pitch one more out. From first base, I was a cheerleader for Andy.

"How slow do you have to throw it to get a strike in there?" I said.

"Pretty slow," Andy said.

"Do it."

He took a slow wind up and just tossed the ball toward the plate. It was so slow the batter didn't know what to do with it. He took it for a strike. "Same thing!" I hollered, not even trying to hide it.

He threw the slow strike again, and the hitter smashed a line drive foul down the third base line. One and two.

"Waste one," I said, "but don't throw it away."

"What do you mean?"

"Time!" I called.

I ran to the mound. "You're ahead of him. Just wing one in there. You can waste one. Just don't lose him after that. We'll have to come back with the slow strike after that."

"So I should just fire away?"

37

"Just once. But don't let it get past Jimmy, or we're down by two."

He nodded. He took a gigantic wind-up, fired the ball, and followed through. It split the heart of the plate, and the startled batter just stood staring as the umpire called him out.

We might have been more excited if we hadn't been down one in the bottom of an extra inning. We hurried off the field.

Marty, the left-hander, was now at first base. The reliever was a big kid, probably their best pitcher. They needed to save this lead and move on, so they figured it was worth an inning of his time.

Jack led off with a major league foul ball behind the plate that their catcher somehow hauled in. Fortunately, Ryan was coming up. He was overdue. He singled down the right field line. Now we were in business. Brent sacrifice bunted him to second, so our future rode with him there and two outs. Jimmy was up.

I was confident Jimmy could get a hit to drive him in, though their pitcher was good and fast. That's Jimmy's kind of pitching. I noticed a crowd gathering in our stands. The other game was over. Park City kids were trudging away with their parents, while the Beach team and their fans gathered at our game. Beach was highly rated. It would be fun to face them if we got that far.

My heart sank when Jimmy was walked intentionally so they could have a force at either base and pitch to Andy, our ninth hitter. I looked at the end of the bench where Matt and Kyle sat, both staring at me, eager and willing to pinch hit. I couldn't do that to Andy. He deserved a chance.

"Whatever you do," I told him, "take the first pitch."

I flashed the sign for a double steal. Both runners acknowledged that they had caught the sign, but each looked puzzled. It was risky and maybe stupid, but I had to get rid of that force possibility. If Andy got the bat on the ball, it wasn't going far, and I sure didn't want to lose the game because Andy grounded into a force out.

On the other hand, if Lake County was smart enough to ignore Ryan and tried to throw Jimmy out at second, they could probably do it, he was that slow. My guess was that they wouldn't risk throwing to either base with the game on the line. Andy had done nothing against Marty, so I'm sure they thought their ace could get him out.

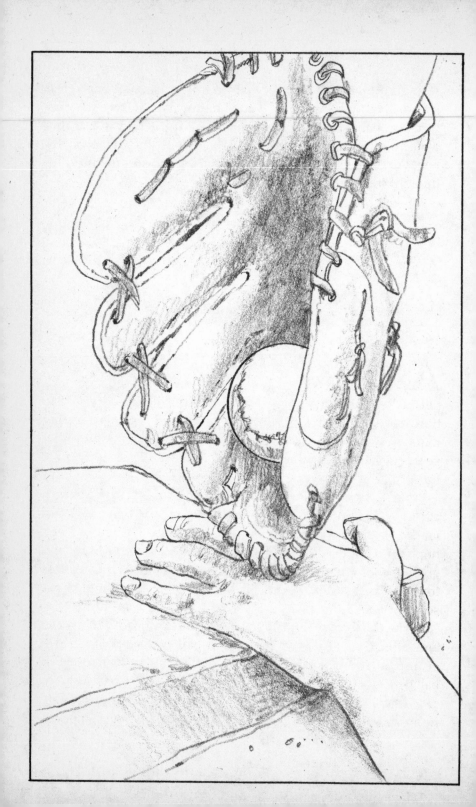

5

The Big Finish

Andy took the first pitch, and Ryan and Jimmy took off. The catcher caught the fastball on the outside of the plate, in a perfect position to throw. He stood and faked a throw, not to third but to second, and for an instant I had a sinking feeling that Jimmy and our team were history. But the catcher never let go of the ball, both runners moved up, and the stage was set for Andy.

He stood in there with a one and oh count, staring straight at the pitcher and never once looking to me for a sign. Had he looked, I would have given him the take sign. If there was any hope for us, it was that Andy could somehow coax a walk and give Cory another chance. Even though this new pitcher was tough, I knew Cory could get the bat on the ball and make something happen.

The next pitch sailed high over Andy's head. He swung and missed what would have been ball two, and our bench erupted. "Wait for your pitch, Andy! That should have been ball two!"

That's not the smartest thing to say to a weak hitter. First he's going up there to become a hero, to do whatever you say, to try to drive in the tying run. Then I tell him to take, so he takes a ball. Now he figures he has a chance to win the game, so he swings at a bad pitch. Everybody hollers at him for that, so now he's afraid to swing. The next pitch is right down the middle, and of course Andy is now afraid to swing and takes it for strike two.

I called time out and called him over to the first base coach's box where I stood.

"Andy, listen," I said, "you swung at a bad pitch. Don't worry about it. You can't take any more close ones with two strikes. If it's way over your head or in the dirt or if it's way outside or almost hits you, lay off it. But if it's close enough to reach it might be close enough to call for a strike. If you strike out swinging, then you did the best you could, but if you take a called third strike, that's like not even trying. Understand?"

He nodded, but I could see he was scared to death.

"Andy, you're not just trying to keep from striking out. You're trying to drive the ball somewhere and at least get that tying run in. It's unlikely he's gonna throw you three more balls for a walk now, so look for a pitch that's close and go for it."

"Let's go, boys!" the umpire shouted.

Andy went back to the plate, looking very determined and very nervous. The next pitch nearly hit him, but he still almost swung at it.

That scared me but also encouraged me. I wouldn't have given a nickel for our chances right then, but I would have hated to see him get called out on strikes.

The two and two pitch was a little high but reachable. Andy took a huge cut at it and fouled it back over the screen. I was dying. I clapped. "C'mon, Andy! You can do it!"

Why hadn't I thought to have him try to bunt? We had succeeded almost every time we had bunted that night, and that might have been the only way Andy could get the bat on the ball. Well, it was too late now. I didn't want him bunting with two strikes. There was nothing more any of us could do for Andy. It was up to him. The game was his.

The Lake County right-hander looked in hard and long for the signal and the target. I saw the catcher put one finger down, heard Jimmy holler from second, "Fastball, Andy!" as if that made any difference, and saw the catcher set up on the outside corner. The pitcher wound up, Ryan danced up the line off third, Jimmy crept off second. Here came the pitch, hard, low, and on that outside corner. Andy stepped into it and drove it hard, on a line, into right center field.

I stood there with my mouth open, watching the ball bounce once and hit the fence, the right fielder and the center fielder flying madly after it. I knew Ryan had scored already and that Jimmy was chugging around third. All Andy had to do was reach first, and we had won.

He sprinted up the line, his mouth open, his eyes glued to the right fielder picking up the ball. As I watched in horror, Andy made the mistake of making a turn toward second rather than just running through the single that would have given us the game. That would have been OK too, once both runs had scored, because even if Andy got tagged at second, it wouldn't mean anything. The game would have been over. But he missed first!

With his eyes on the outfielder, he had completely missed the bag, and Marty, the left-hander who had started on the mound for Lake County and was now playing first, saw it. He had backed up to near the mound to line up on the relay from the outfield to the plate in an attempt to get Jimmy at home, and he had seen Andy miss first. Worse, the infield umpire had seen it too.

The throw came in high from right field, and the play at the plate might have been close. But even though the catcher was hollering at Marty to let the throw go through, the big first baseman leaped and caught the ball. He knew if he could tag first before Andy did, neither run would count. It would be three outs on a force at first, and Lake County would win.

Meanwhile I was screaming myself hoarse. "Andy! You gotta get back, get back, get back!"

Andy had skidded to a stop just past half way to second, stumbled trying to turn around, and was now charging back. And here came Marty on the dead run, ball tucked securely in his glove. The umpire moved into position for a good view. The Baker Street bench was mobbing Jimmy, thinking we had won, not knowing what was going on at first base.

Marty made a grave error. He must have thought he had a better chance of beating Andy to the bag by cutting him off early and tagging him, rather than just tagging the bag for the force. I saw both guys hurtling toward first, and I dropped to my knees and pointed to the bag. "Down, Andy! Down!"

Andy dove headfirst toward the bag, keeping his body away from the diving Marty, who lunged at him with the ball in his outstretched glove. I could tell that if Marty had dived straight for the base, he would have beat Andy, and we'd have lost. As it was, both players dove too early. Andy wound up a few inches short of the bag, and Marty wound up a few inches short of Andy.

The umpire, crouched and ready, stared at the two boys, studying their positions and making no call. As if moving in front of a mirror, the boys hunched themselves up onto one knee for a final thrust, Marty toward Andy, Andy toward the bag. To me it looked like a tie, Marty slapping his glove on Andy's arm as Andy touched the base.

The umpire leaped and came down shouting and signaling. "He's safe! He's safe! He's safe!"

Our Baker Street teammates raced out and lifted Andy onto their shoulders. He couldn't stop grinning. It took me awhile to get them to calm down and line up to shake hands with the other team.

We were still jumping around and carrying on when we got to the parking lot. Traci Kent's friend Jill had sped on ahead to tell Traci, who jumped out of the car to see what was going on. Kyle, our know-it-all who doesn't play well but knows every detail of the game, was explaining everything.

"Interestingly," he was saying, "in fact maybe even ironically, Andy not only drove in the tying and winning runs, but he was also the winning pitcher. He was the pitcher of record when the winning run was scored."

"How about that?" Traci said over and over. "How about that?"

Before everybody split up I told the guys, "We play Highland tomorrow night on the other field. Be here on time!"

Traci asked Andy how he was getting home, and he said he had his bike. She turned to Jill. "Can we give Dallas a ride home? I need to talk to him."

Jill shrugged. "Sure. Why not? Just don't tell anybody we took a guy home from a ball game and he was twelve!"

We all laughed.

"Can you ride with us?" Traci asked.

"I guess."

"Well, don't sound so excited."

The fact is, I was excited. But I thought I should probably let my parents know first. Oh, well, I had walked to the game. They wouldn't worry if I didn't ride home with them, as long as I wasn't late. I rode in the backseat behind Jill. Traci sat on the passenger's side in the front and turned in the seat to talk to me.

"I guess I was a little hard on you, Dallas, especially when I was wrong. I shouldn't have accused you of doing something to Andy on purpose."

"Thanks. I wouldn't do that."

"I guess I should know that, but after what he did to you and Jimmy and Matt, most people would have wanted to get back at him. Why don't you?"

"Oh, part of me does," I admitted. "But I know that's not right. I want to try to treat people the way I would want them to treat me."

"I get it. The Golden Rule."

"Yeah, I guess it's the Golden Rule. I got it from the Bible."

"Andy told me you were a churchy type."

"I don't know about that. I go to church, but I don't know what a churchy type is."

"You don't? It's someone who lives by the Bible and all that."

"Anything wrong with that?"

"I guess not," she said. "But it is churchy. I don't think I could add another set of rules to my life."

I didn't say anything. I was curious and wondered what she meant by that, but it didn't seem like the thing a kid asks a high school sophomore, and she was sure making me feel young.

"I like to do what's right," I blurted. "I didn't think I would at first, and I didn't always like to. In fact, I don't always do what's right, but I feel better when I do."

She nodded seriously. "Doing right is prison," she said.

I didn't understand that at all. Again, I wanted to ask what she meant, but she was sort of saying this stuff in a way that didn't invite questions, if you know what I mean.

She changed the subject so quickly, I almost missed it. "I appreciate you giving Andy the chance to be a hero once."

"I wish I could take credit for it," I said. "But his turn to hit came up, and he had to come through. And he did."

"But how did you work it out that he would become the winning pitcher, with all those pitchers you used? I mean, how many of your players pitched in that game?"

"More than half. There are eleven of us on the team, nine played, and six pitched to at least one hitter. Frankly, I wasn't thinking about Andy being the last one and getting the win in case we scored. When he allowed a run, off of one of Toby's runners that is, I didn't think we had a chance. I sure didn't think he'd get the game winning RBI and be the winning pitcher."

We pulled into my driveway. My parents weren't home yet. "Let's take a walk," she said. "You mind waiting, Jill?"

Jill shook her head, pulled a textbook off the seat beside her, and settled back to read. Traci headed out between our shed and the barn. The bulb in front of the barn provided the only light, and I wondered what my parents would think of my walking our property in the dark with a great looking sophomore.

6

Fat?!

I needn't have worried. Traci stopped under the barn light and leaned against the wall. "The truth is, Dallas, I knew all about your church and the way you live and all that because it's all Andy talks about. He knows I've been worried sick about cheerleader tryouts the day after tomorrow, and he thinks I should talk to you about it. I don't mean to make you feel bad, but I frankly don't know what I'm doing here, except that I appreciate Andy caring enough to suggest it."

"Why should that make me feel bad?"

"Because if you knew the truth, I think I should have my head examined before I talk to a twelve-year-old about my problems."

I agreed but didn't say so. I was nervous. "What are your problems?" I said.

"Just that I've gained so much weight since last year that I might as well not even try out this year."

I scowled and shook my head. "You've gained weight?"

"I sure have. I'm fat."

I thought she was kidding. I didn't want to be rude enough to back up a step and check her out, but I had never seen an ounce of fat on her or any of her friends, especially the cheerleaders. Some of them were a little stockier or more solid than others, but Traci wasn't one of those. I would have said she was in perfect shape. Not heavy at all, not skinny. Just right. Athletic.

"You're not fat," I said, not intending to encourage her but just to state a fact.

For some reason, what I said offended her. She bristled. "That shows how much you know! You don't have to say that just to make me feel better. You can see like anybody else that Jill is much thinner than I am. She won't have any trouble making the squad, and she'll probably be captain."

"Everybody around school thinks it's going to be you."

I guess I shouldn't have said that. With her back to the wall, Traci slammed her fists on the barn behind her, making me jump. "It's not going to be me! Why should I humiliate myself by trying out and getting cut?"

I turned and looked self-consciously toward Jill's car. She still sat there reading under the inside light.

My parents pulled in and parked. Mom called to me on her way to the house. "What're you doing, Dallas?"

"Just talking to Traci Kent."

"Oh, hi, Traci!" Mom said.

Traci waved and smiled.

"Dallas, you'd better come in, in twenty minutes or so! School tomorrow!"

"OK!"

"I'm sorry I got you in trouble," Traci said.

"What do you mean? I'm not in trouble."

"Oh, yes, you are. I can tell. She's gonna give it to you when you get inside."

I snorted. "No, she's not."

Traci looked amazed. I couldn't figure out this girl. I had never really talked to her before, other than just to say hi. Now she was saying all kinds of confusing things, and I couldn't keep up with her.

"Anyway," she said, "as of right now, I'm not trying out, so if you think you can talk me into it, this is your last chance."

I got a crazy idea. Since I didn't know what was going on inside her head, maybe it would be OK if she didn't know what was going on inside of mine either. "What do I care what you do?" I said, trying not to sound unkind. "If you don't want to try out, don't try out."

I stunned her. She stared at me, then started slowly toward the car.

"Wait a minute," I said.

When she turned back her eyes were full of tears. "I was just trying to get a rise out of you. What's the matter?"

"You don't get it, do you?"

"Get what?"

"Get my problem."

"No, I guess I don't. I guess you're not kidding about thinking you're fat and saying you're not going to try out for cheerleading because you're afraid you'll get cut. I thought maybe you were fishing for a compliment."

I wasn't getting far. She looked more and more shocked. I plunged ahead. "All right, I'll tell you what I think. You must be serious, but you're way off. Everybody I know thinks you're gorgeous and the best cheerleader they've ever seen. If, for some reason, you don't want to try out, then you'll never know if the judges agree. I'm tellin' you, Traci, even the other cheerleaders think you're going to be captain—even the seniors—and they're happy about it. What do your parents think?"

She spun around lightly and sat down, leaning back against the barn. "My parents," she said flatly. "How would I know?"

"You don't talk to them?"

"They don't talk to me."

"Are you serious?"

"Oh, they talk, but they don't really talk directly to me about me, if you know what I mean."

"I'm sorry, I don't."

She shifted uncomfortably. "All I ever hear from them is how cute or how talented or how smart or how thin or how in shape my friends are."

"Maybe they mean that as a compliment to you. You choose good friends."

"Give me a break. I get the message loud and clear. I'm ugly, I'm a klutz, I'm dumb, and I'm fat."

I sat looking at her. Was she serious? How could a person say something like that about herself, especially when it was so untrue? "Could I take those one at a time?" I asked.

She shrugged. "Whatever."

"Ugly?"

She nodded. "I don't even like to spend much time looking in the mirror."

"How do you explain everybody telling you all the time how cute you look? Or the guys always staring at you?"

"People tell me that to make me feel better about my funny looking nose and my fat."

Her nose turned up in a cute, cheerleader-type of a way. I was finding this all very hard to believe. "Uh-huh."

"And whenever I catch anybody looking at me I assume I have a run in my stocking or that my mascara is running."

"How does a klutz get to be a cheerleader?"

She didn't hesitate. "Luck," she said. "I knew the right people. But now with the new girls and my extra weight, my luck has run out."

"Forget the weight for a minute; let's talk about how dumb you are."

"Let's not. It's embarrassing."

I laughed. I shouldn't have. It made her cry again. "Hey, Traci! Look, I guess I don't know how to talk to high school girls. I'm sorry. I'm not trying to make you cry. It's just that I don't understand any of this. I know you made the high honor roll all four quarters last year, and—"

"Three."

"Three what?"

"Three quarters. The third quarter I was on the regular honor roll."

"My mistake. So three out of four on the high honor roll and one on the regular honor roll?"

"Right, but don't you see? I'm not smart. In fact, I'm the opposite. That's why I have to work so hard, and then I get on the honor roll with people who really are smart, and I'm a phony."

"There's nothing phony about getting straight A's, which is the only way to get on the high honor roll."

"But I had more A-minuses than anyone on that list. Four of my seven A's were minuses, and only one was a plus, and that was physical education."

"Which proves you're not a klutz."

"Oh, they hand out A-pluses to cheerleaders. It doesn't mean anything."

"Anyway, what's wrong with an A-minus?"

"It just shows how lucky I was, and remember, I was working my tail off to get even that."

"Even that," I repeated flatly. "Let's get back to the fat part."

"Oh, please."

"Are you a little taller than you were last year?"

"An inch."

"So if you hadn't gained any weight, you'd probably look like a string bean."

"I'd love to look like a string bean! That's exactly what I want to look like! That's what Jill looks like."

"Aha!" I said.

"Aha what?"

"I've finally caught you. I know what your problem is."

"You do?"

"I do. You're blind!" I laughed. I thought that was pretty funny—and true in its own way. "If you think Jill looks like a string bean, you're blind! She looks the same as you."

"I wish."

"She does! She's a little taller, but you have the same—you know—build."

"I wish."

"You do!"

"Talk about blind, Dallas. How you could compare a thin, perfect, athletic body like Jill's to a fat, roly-poly person like me is beyond me."

She stood, as if to leave.

"Traci, wait a minute. Please."

She stopped and turned around. "Help me," she said. "Tell me something that will help me."

"I've tried. You're talking nonsense, but you don't want to hear that."

"It doesn't surprise me. What else could a person like me talk?"

"Now you're begging for me to disagree."

She sighed. Then shook her head. "I don't know," she said. "I just don't know. I can't keep up with the pressure."

Now I thought she was getting closer to the truth. I could understand how trying out for cheerleading could bring pressure, and having everybody think you were going to be captain would make it worse. Especially if you didn't believe in yourself. I said nothing.

"What are you thinking?" she asked.

I didn't know what to say. "I, uh, I guess I'm not sure. I was sort of wondering what you would do if you did try out and made it and were named captain."

"That would be the worst," she said.

Now I was really confused. I thought all this poor-me stuff was just to cover in case she didn't reach the goal she desperately wanted. Now she was saying that making it would be worse? I must have looked puzzled but didn't say anything.

"I'd be the biggest hypocrite on the earth," she said. "I don't deserve that. I wouldn't be able to explain it or live up to it. Jill, or somebody like her, should be captain. I shouldn't even be on the squad."

The scary part was, she had finally convinced me that she really believed that. What had happened to this beautiful, talented, smart, trim girl to make her think she was ugly, a klutz, stupid, and fat?

7

The Semifinals

I thought I had blown it with Traci because I had not known what to say or how to say it. I had upset her, I knew that, and it wouldn't have surprised me if she never wanted to talk to me again. That would have been all right with me. I mean, I didn't want to have an enemy, but what did I know about giving advice to high school girls?

That's why I was surprised when Traci showed up at our game the next night and asked if she could talk to me again later.

"Sure," I said, "but I don't know when."

"How about tonight, after the game?"

"I can't. This is a late game, and I have school tomorrow."

"How about now?"

"I can't. I'm in charge of batting and infield practice."

She looked so disappointed and sad that I felt guilty. I didn't know why. It wasn't like she was my responsibility. Why didn't she talk to her girl friends, or guys her age, or a teacher, or a counselor, or her parents?

"You know, Traci, the Saturday game is at four, and then there's some pee-wee softball tournament. I'm staying to watch that. Maybe you could stay too, and we can talk."

"That'd be nice, but that won't help me make my decision about the tryouts Friday."

"You haven't decided yet?"

She shook her head.

From a distance someone shouted, "Let's go, O'Neil! Flirt later!"

That's just what I was afraid of. Traci was cute and everything, but I never even dreamed of liking her as a girl friend. She was too old, too much to hope for. It had never entered my head, except that I was afraid other people would think it had. And now they did think that. Grief.

"You've got to go," she said. "Just tell me what you think I should do."

"I think you should make your own decision," I said.

"You're no help. I want to know what you would do if you were me."

"I'd wonder how a guy got into the cheerleading tryouts."

For the first time since we'd been talking, I saw Traci smile. In fact, she laughed. It would be the last time I would see that.

"Really, what would you do?"

"Well," I said, "I sure wouldn't quit before I got started."

"You'd try out?"

"Of course."

"C'mon, O'Neil!" someone shouted. "Now or never!"

As I dragged our equipment bag to the dugout, I saw the highly favored and first-seeded Deerfield team heading for the other diamond. I was certain we would probably face those giants if we got past Highland. They were the biggest kids our age I had ever seen. They won the night before with their weakest pitcher, and we heard they were saving their best guy for the championship.

We went with our usual line-up against Highland, a team of mostly small, scrappy players and a pitcher who threw knuckleballs, pitches that danced and swept with the wind and were almost impossible to hit. We were the home team again, though if we won we would be the visitors against the winner of the other bracket in the final on Saturday.

The only change I made was that Bugsy would start pitching this time, with Cory pitching the third and fourth and me finishing. That put me at short and Cory at second to start. I hoped Bugsy could hold Highland a little better than Cory might, giving us a chance to get a little lead. That way we could change the way Highland played and the way their pitcher pitched, and Cory's job would be to keep a lead rather than hold them to nothing while we tried to get on the board.

It might have worked all right, if Bugsy had been sharp and the knuckleballer not so sharp. By the time Cory came in to pitch in the top of the third, we were down 2-0, and our first six hitters had been retired in a row. Cory and I had struck out, both chasing three straight fluttering pitches that looked slow and fat and then darted toward the dirt.

Toby also struck out to lead off the top of the second, and though Jack and Ryan got bats on the ball, one popped out and the other grounded back to the pitcher. I was worried. After a scoreless first inning, Bugsy had given up a two-run double to their number seven hitter.

Cory was pretty tough, holding them scoreless in his first half-inning despite facing the top of their order. Brent and Jimmy walked to lead off the bottom of the third, but Cory struck out, and Bugsy hit into a double play on a liner to first. Though we had spoiled Knuckles's perfect game, he still had a no-hitter going. And of course, we still trailed.

Highland scored another run in the top of the fourth on a towering, two-out homer by the same guy who had hit the double earlier. I wondered how he got stuck in the seventh spot in their order, but then I thought of Jimmy, whom we put at eighth, even though he was one of the better hitters on our team. Of course, we put our best home run hitter, Ryan, sixth too. I wanted to keep that seventh hitter in mind for the last two innings. I had to be able to keep them scoreless for us to have any chance, and we were going to have to strike soon to be in the game at all.

It happened in the bottom of the fourth. I knew we needed base runners even more than we needed big hits, so I told everybody to wait this pitcher out. I wondered if he could throw strikes if he had to. Every pitch he threw me looked good when it started but was out of the strike zone by the time it passed the plate, and I walked.

Toby took a strike, then three straight balls. I gave him the take sign, and he took another strike. He glared at me, but I tried to encourage him, shouting that we needed him on base. He walked on the next pitch. After Jack struck out, I called time and ran in to talk to Ryan, something the umpires usually frown on but which they allowed because we didn't have a coach.

"Did you notice what he did when he fell behind in the count?" I asked Ryan.

"I sure did. He forgets about the knuckler and just lays it in there—or tries."

"Yeah, and he's got nothin' on the ball. I think we figured out why he throws the knuckler. It's all he's got. Listen, be real selective as long as he's throwing that flutter ball, but you've got the hit sign all the way when he falls behind in the count, no matter what the count is."

"Are you serious? No matter what?"

I nodded and ran back to second base.

Ryan stepped in and immediately found himself ahead in the count two and oh. The Highland pitcher switched to a straight pitch, but Ryan was a little over-eager and chased it out of the strike zone for a foul ball, two and one.

I flashed the steal sign to Toby at first, who looked surprised. I nodded to assure him I was serious.

Though still behind the hitter, Knuckles went back to his favorite pitch. Ryan, showing great discipline and patience, held up his swing in time to see it run in on him for ball three. Toby and I were off with the pitch. The catcher fired to third, a little high or I'd have been out. That told me he had the arm to have thrown Toby out easily at second, but they were wisely trying for the shorter throw and to get the lead runner.

Now the pitcher couldn't afford ball four. He didn't want the tying run on base. Ryan twisted his rubber cleats into the dirt and set himself, hands at the end of the bat. He was pretty sure what was coming, and so was I.

Normally in a situation like that I like to distract the pitcher by dancing off third base and running half way down the line. Now I just stood on the bag. I couldn't risk getting picked off by pitcher or catcher, and I wanted this guy to concentrate on nothing but getting the ball over.

He wound and pitched a straight ball with nothing on it, right at the outside corner of the plate. Ryan was ready for it. He stepped, reached out, and swung with those quick, powerful little wrists of his, and drove the ball deep to left. The left fielder just turned and watched it sky over the fence. We had broken up the no-hitter and the shutout, not to mention erasing the lead with one swing. We mobbed Ryan when he reached the plate.

The best thing was, we still had just one out. Knuckles was rattled, and we were ready to pounce. Brent walked, and Jimmy doubled him in. When Andy came up, I sneaked a peek at his sister who had been watching from her usual spot in the front row. As he approached the plate she buried her face in her hands and waited until he singled before she looked up and applauded. That pushed Jimmy in, and Cory doubled him in. By the time Bugsy got up, we led 6-3 with one out and a man at second.

Knuckles was history, and they brought in one of the slowest pitchers we'd faced all season. I guess they'd used their ace in the first game, and when we caught onto their second best guy, they were left without much.

Bugsy tripled to make it 7-3, and their shortstop made an error on my grounder, so I reached second while Bugs scored.

Toby drove one off the right field wall, and while the outfielders and infielders threw it all over the place, Highland's hopes died and Toby and I circled the bases to make it 10-3.

Jack homered, and Ryan flied out deep to left, just missing his second homer in the same inning. With two outs, Brent hit an inside-the-park home run, his first homer of the season. Jimmy followed with a shot over the center field fence, and suddenly it was over.

What had begun as a perfect game, then a no-hitter, then a shutout, was suddenly a big loss for Highland. If either team is leading by ten or more at the end of four innings, the game is over.

We had not only won, but we had also sent a message to the winner of the other semifinal, probably Deerfield, that we were fearful hitters. It may not have been true; we'd had our troubles with good pitching, and Deerfield had a bunch of that, but winning by ten in four innings sure made us look good.

Our game was over so early that, after shaking hands with Highland and gathering up our stuff, we went to watch the Deerfield-Beach game. I was having a good time with my friends and scouting Deerfield when I realized I was being watched. I turned and saw someone looking at me from a seat two or three rows up behind us. It was Traci. I smiled weakly at her. She scowled at me. What now?

I turned back to my friends, glancing back occasionally. Every time I checked, Traci was giving me a dirty look. I decided to ignore that but go back to see her anyway. I stayed in my good mood and climbed up next to her.

"Hi!" I said.

She turned away.

"What's wrong?" I said, wondering why I was wasting my time.

"I thought you weren't going to have time for me after the game," she said coldly.

My mouth fell open. What was this all about? It was almost as if I had a nagging wife like my Uncle Kirby has. He just quit talking to her to keep from saying or doing the wrong thing. What was I supposed to do?

"Our game got over early," I said, with enough irritation in my voice to show her that I didn't think I had to explain anything to her. "I thought we agreed we would talk after Saturday's game."

"That's too late! Don't you see? It'll all be over by then. I will have tried out and been humiliated, but I won't know yet whether I made it or or not."

"Captain, you mean."

"At all, I mean. I wouldn't even want to be captain, and I've already told you why not."

I sighed. "Traci, all I can tell you is, you should make your own decisions. If you're leaving it up to me, which isn't fair, I say try out, do your best, and let the judges decide who makes it, who should be captain."

"If you say so," she said, and somehow I hated the sound of that.

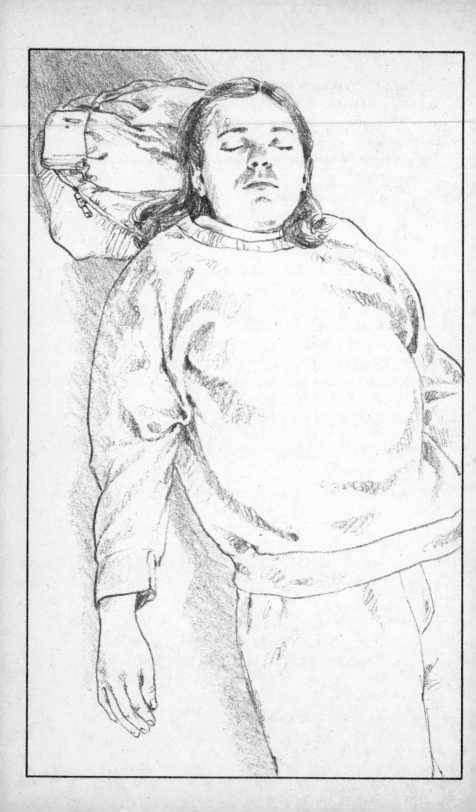

8

The Tryouts

Jimmy Calabresi was still pouting because he thought I had been ignoring him lately. I tried to tell him that I had simply had a lot on my mind with the tournament, Andy, Traci, and everything, but that didn't seem to encourage him. I told him the whole story about Traci and invited him to go with me to the high school after our school day was over.

"To watch cheerleader tryouts? That sounds boring."

"Well," I said, "I'm going, so if you want to spend time with me, that's where I'll be."

Jimmy shrugged. "I guess if you make it sound so dramatic, it'll be all right."

"It ought to be good. Traci's playin' this poor-me-I'm-no-good bit, but everybody I know says she'll make it easily and be named captain."

"I saw her cheer at freshman games last year," Jimmy said. "She's better than anybody on the varsity last year."

"This tryout is for the varsity. You have to be at least a sophomore to try out, but you can't cheer on the freshman squad again if you don't make the varsity."

"So this is it, do or die."

"Well, I wouldn't make it sound that bad, but it is like a single-elimination tournament."

We walked past the junior high and on up the street to the big high school. I didn't expect what I saw in the auxiliary gym where the tryouts were to be held. There must have been fifty girls waiting for their chance to try out. Behind a table sat a couple of men and four women with clipboards. One stood to make an announcement.

"We'll look at each of you one at a time. By now you all should have learned at least one of our basic cheers. Do whichever you want, then do a C-jump, a V-jump, and a split if you can. Don't worry if you can't do a complete split. Finish by encouraging the crowd to cheer, and picture us as the crowd. We'll go in alphabetical order. Anderson!"

A short, pudgy, blonde girl skipped to the center of the floor and began a basic cheer so slowly that it almost made us laugh. Her face showed severe concentration as she tried to remember what words went with which moves. When she finished and did her two jumps and splits, she hardly left the ground. She did, however, do a complete split. When she encouraged the "crowd" to cheer, she just shouted, "C'mon, you guys! Yell!" Then she laughed self-consciously and ran off.

The panel of judges smiled courteously, and the chief judge told her to watch the bulletin board Monday morning.

As girl after girl made her way past the judges, I looked for Traci Kent. The girls who had been on the squad the year before and several former freshman cheerleaders stood limbering up in their uniforms. They looked nervous, but confident. They bent and stretched and practiced their moves. Other girls tried to do the same, but they looked terribly self-conscious and mostly just made themselves warm and sweaty.

The first veteran to try out was Jill, who made the ones before her look pretty weak, or maybe it as the other way around: they had been so unimpressive that Jill looked all the better. She was precise, athletic, pretty, and loud, and when she encouraged the panel to cheer, they did! It was incredible. They clapped and yelled, then suddenly composed themselves again, as if embarrassed at their outburst.

We heard a lot of girls whispering about her being an automatic choice, maybe even captain. She was a junior and had made the squad the year before. When some mentioned her shot at the captain spot, others mentioned Traci's name, and that's when I got my first glimpse of her. I almost didn't see her, but I wondered about the reaction of the rest of the spectators. I swung around to look at everyone else, and there was Traci, alone, on the top row of the bleachers, her back to the wall, staring at the competition.

Her chin was in her hands, and she looked stiff, unsmiling. I wondered if she had signed up to try out or was just watching. I would know when they got to the K's. Quite a few of the veteran cheerleaders had names in the first half of the alphabet, and each made the other hopefuls look a little less hopeful. There was a sophomore or two with promise, and one girl who looked excellent turned out to be a transfer from another school where she had been a cheerleader.

Most of the rest were pretty plain to my untrained eyes. I thought I could tell when the judges liked someone. They sat forward on their chairs, leaning into the competitor, making their notes later. When they didn't like someone, they looked over the tops of their glasses and took notes during the routines.

I hadn't thought about what Traci was wearing until her name was called, the gym grew silent, and she slowly moved down from the top row. Every eye was on her, and she was not wearing a cheerleading outfit. She wore a sweatshirt over leotards, and sneakers. She had not warmed up or stretched. She looked scared.

Traci walked slowly to the center of the floor and stood facing the judges with a why-am-I-here look. Then she broke into a standard cheer. There were a few flashes of her ability, but mostly she looked tired and tight. Her jumps were low, and her shoes dragged on the floor. The longer she went the worse she looked and the more panic-stricken she looked.

"She's history," Jimmy hissed before I shushed him.

"Let's watch her two jumps and splits."

Her jumps didn't look any better than anyone else's and quite a bit less impressive than the other former cheerleaders'. When she did the splits she had to bounce to get all the way down, then she toppled over. She quickly jumped to her feet and looked awkward. She looked pained and embarrassed, and she forgot to encourage the "crowd."

As she shuffled off, looking near tears, the chief judge said sweetly, "Traci, encourage us to cheer."

As if in a dream, Traci stepped back and moved into a standard cheerleading jump. "Yell, everyone! Yell!"

It was weak, and it was embarrassing. No one clapped. No one cheered. The judges stared at her with sympathy and then looked at each other, slowly writing notes. Traci had humiliated herself just as she feared, and she left the gym looking half her normal size. No one followed her. No one looked at her but me.

As she moved breathlessly through the door into the hall, I leaned out of the bleachers and saw her stumble. She almost hit the floor but righted herself and staggered to where she leaned against the wall.

"Wait here," I told Jimmy. "I'll be right back."

I bounded down the bleachers and quickly approached Traci.

"Are you all right?"

She nodded and looked away. "I—uh—I uh—I knew this would—um—" and she slumped to the floor. I tried to catch her, but she was too heavy for me.

I looked around frantically, but everyone else was in the gym. I didn't know what to do. Her head had hit the floor, but I couldn't tell if it had been hard enough to knock her out or if she had been out before she hit the floor. I whipped off my jacket and bundled it up under her head. I had seen people slap fainting victims on TV and in films, but I was afraid to hit her very hard. I barely nudged her cheek a few times, and she opened her eyes. They seemed to be rolling back in her head. I wished I hadn't asked Jimmy to stay put. I needed him.

Fortunately, he was a curious kid, and in a few seconds he came looking for me.

"Jimmy, go see if anyone's in the nurse's office."

"Where's that?"

"I don't know! Ask someone!"

"What happened?"

"Ask me later! Go!"

He ran off.

I slapped Traci a little harder, and her eyes opened again. I knew this was more than disappointment. She was weak and dizzy and had fainted, but why?

A couple of girls left the gym and screamed when they saw me bending over Traci, cradling her head. "What happened?" they cried.

"She fainted. Do you go to this school?"

"Is she going to be all right?"

"I don't know! She needs help! Do you go here or not?"

"Yes! Why?"

"Find the nurse! My friend just ran that way looking for her."

They looked where I was pointing, and suddenly they didn't seem to care anymore. "He went the right way," one said. "He'll find her."

I couldn't believe it when they walked back into the gym. How could I have known they were going to tell a bunch of their friends and that I would have to deal with a crowd? Within seconds I was surrounded by people jockeying for a better view. Luckily, the school nurse, a stocky woman in her fifties, came pounding down the hall, bellowing that everybody should get out of her way.

"You a friend of hers?" the woman asked. Her nameplate read "Betty Bolla, R.N."

I nodded. "I don't know what happened to her though."

"She just fainted?"

"Yup. She had just had her cheerleader tryout."

Nurse Bolla nodded, checked Traci's pulse, and felt her face. "I'm not a doctor," she said, "but this girl is cold and peaked. Do you know her well enough to know if she's eaten recently?"

I shook my head, puzzled. "She's been talking about being too fat."

The nurse, who had been on her knees, rocked back onto her heels, still squatting like a catcher. "That's what I was afraid of," she said. "These crazy girls starve themselves till they're too weak to function. Listen, did she hit her head hard? Is that what knocked her out?"

"I don't know. If I had to guess, I think she was out before she fell."

Miss Bolla pulled a small packet of smelling salts from her pocket, broke it open and waved it beneath Traci's nose. I was a few feet away, and it was foul. Traci stirred.

"Up you go, girl," the nurse said. "Come with me."

Traci struggled to her feet with our help, and we walked her down two corridors to the nurse's office. I was surprised at how gruff the nurse sounded, once she had Traci's attention.

"When did you eat last, Miss Kent?" she said.

"I don't know."

"Yes, you do! Now if you want to starve yourself to death, that's your business, but my business is to get you off these premises and to your home in some reasonable state of health. Now tell me when you ate last and what you ate."

"I don't remember," Traci whined.

"Yes, you do! Are you hungry?"

"No!"

"Yeah, I'll bet. Did you eat today?"

"I think so."

"I'll bet not. What did you have?"

"I don't know. Something for breakfast."

"What? What did you have?"

"I don't know."

The nurse bent down over Traci who sat in a chair at a desk. "You, lady, you are going to tell me what you had to eat today, and you are going to tell me the truth. Otherwise, I'll get a doctor in here to force-feed you some hypo-carbohydrate and sugar mixture and have you admitted to a hospital, psychiatric or otherwise."

9

The Problem

That got Traci's attention. "You're not really gonna force-feed me and have me committed, are you?"

"You know I will," Nurse Bolla said, "unless you tell me right now what you had for breakfast."

"Celery."

"How much?"

"One stalk."

"How big?"

"Three, four inches."

"Anything to drink?"

Traci shook her head.

"That's what I was afraid of. What'd you have yesterday?"

Traci pursed her lips and shook her head.

"Tell me."

She shook her head again.

"You're telling me you had nothing to eat yesterday and a tiny stalk of celery today?"

"It's my business," Traci said.

"Until you collapse in my hallway it's your business," the nurse said. "Now it's my business. Up on the scale."

Traci slowly moved to the scale where the nurse measured and weighed her: five-foot two and ninety-five pounds.

"I'm so embarrassed," Traci said.

"You should be," Nurse Bolla said. "You're wasting away."

It was as if Traci hadn't heard her. "I'm so fat."

"Fat? Let me check your records." She went into another room and slid a file drawer open.

Traci looked at me and mouthed again, "Fat! I'm so fat. I hate scales."

"Ninety-five doesn't sound fat to me," I said.

The nurse returned. "Look here. Last year at this time you were five-one and weighed a hundred and five. That was just right. You're small boned. Now you should weigh about one ten."

Traci wasn't listening. "I have to get back to the gym for cheerleader tryouts. I'm trying to make the team."

"They're not posting the results till Monday," I said.

"I still have to try out," she said.

I looked sharply at the nurse, who looked stunned. "I thought you told me she tried out before she fainted."

I nodded, speechless.

"I tried out already? Oh, yeah, 'course I did. I did all right too, huh? Better than you thought I would?"

"I hadn't thought about how you would do," I admitted. "I guess I figured you'd be great."

"And was I?"

I'm glad the nurse interrupted. I wouldn't have known what to say.

"You don't remember trying out?" Miss Bolla said. "I'm calling a doctor."

"No! I'm fine."

"Then you eat this energy bar. In fact, take two. And when you get home, I want you to eat dinner. Do I need to call your mother and make sure you do?"

Suddenly Traci brightened. She tore the wrapping off the energy bar and the smell of carob and protein powder filled the room. She eagerly bit off a chunk and chewed. "You don't need to do that, but I appreciate it. I appreciate all you've done for me and your advice. I'll do better. I promise."

The nurse softened and smiled. "Just eat those, and keep eating. Get your weight and your strength back up, and you'll be a better cheerleader for it. You know starving yourself can be dangerous and addictive. You could become anorexic."

"Thanks again, ma'am," Traci said. And she stood and walked out, looking better than I thought she would.

When we turned a corner Traci dropped the wrapped energy bar and what was left of the unwrapped one in a garbage can, then leaned over it and spit out what she had been chewing. "That tasted good," she said, looking at me. "Now I won't need dinner."

I stopped in mid-stride and let her walk away from me. Then I turned and headed back toward the nurse's office.

Traci spun around in the hall. "Where are you going?" she demanded.

"I'm going to tell the nurse what you just did, what you just said, and what you're planning," I said, hearing my voice echo eerily off the walls. "I know that sounds like a real sixth-grade thing to do, but I'm doin' it anyway! I don't know what else to do."

"I thought you liked me," she said, and her voice was full of wonder and humor, like she was teasing, not accusing.

"I do. That's why I'm doing this."

"Suit yourself." She seemed almost pert, the way she turned and walked away.

I kept watching her, and within a few strides she slowed again and trudged slowly out of the building. I ran to catch up with her. Jimmy had long since left for home.

"Not squealing on me?" she said.

"Yes, I am," I said. "But I was wondering how you're getting home."

"I'm taking the bus," she said.

"Don't you usually ride home with Jill?"

"She drives me, yes. But she's a cheerleader now, and I'm not, so—"

"You don't know that."

"I don't? Don't you? You were there. If they choose me, they'll have to answer to every girl they didn't pick."

What could I say? I knew she was right. "What does that have to do with your friendship with Jill?"

"How can I be friends with a girl who makes me look fat, then beats me out for captain of the cheerleading squad? That's no friendship."

"How do you know she even made the team?"

"Don't be ridiculous."

"And anyway, you said you didn't want to be captain."

"Well, maybe I did. But now I don't even get the chance to turn it down, do I?"

"How do you know?"

"The same way you know, Dallas. You were there. She turned again and began walking away quickly, soon slowing as before.

I could tell she was out of breath. "Are you all right?" I called after her.

"I'm fine," she said over her shoulder.

The nurse's office was dark. She couldn't have been gone long, though. I ran toward the staff parking lot. She was unlocking her car.

I told her all that had happened with Traci.

She sighed and leaned back against her car. "I'm disappointed but not surprised. I deal with a lot more of this than you might imagine."

"I got that feeling by the way you talked to her."

"You have to talk to most of them the same way. They get into this terrible routine of starving themselves to look better or to win some boyfriend or to make the cheerleading squad, and they wind up hurting themselves, falling into eating disorders, and getting really sick."

"What can I do for her?"

"I wish I knew. She looks like a classic candidate for anorexia nervosa."

"What?"

She repeated it.

"What's that?"

"A girl starves herself, thinking she's fat. She can't be convinced otherwise. It's really as much psychological as physiological."

"It's what?"

"It has as much to do with her mind as with her body."

"Really?"

She nodded. "She'll get into a sort of a control trip where food and its intake is the only thing she feels she has a handle on. Though nothing else in her world is right, she can control that. Or she thinks she can. In fact, it'll control her, and it'll kill her if she doesn't get help."

"What kind of help?"

"You want my personal opinion or my professional one?"

"Both!"

"Professionally, she needs medical and psychiatric intervention." She paused, as if realizing she wasn't talking to an adult. "She probably needs to be in a hospital for what she's already done to her body. Five-two and ninety-five pounds doesn't have to be alarming, but having lost weight while increasing in height is a serious matter. You have to do that on purpose. She do pretty bad in the tryouts?"

"Yup."

"Then she won't make the team. Her world will fall apart completely. She'll bury herself in this crusade to get skinny, as if she isn't headed that way already. She could lose a pound a day for a while, and after her body rebels, that will slow down, but not much. You watch, in a month she could lose up to twenty pounds—if she survives."

"You had another opinion?"

"It's personal," she said.

"I don't mind, if you don't."

"Nah, it's just that I could get in trouble talking to you about it in my official capacity, and on school grounds."

"You can tell me. I'm not the type to get people in trouble. I only told you about Traci because I was worried about her."

"Well," she said, shifting her weight and playing with her keys, "I think the child needs God."

That surprised me. I wanted to tell Miss Bolla that I was a Christian and that I agreed, but I was unable to say anything.

She continued. "Just like alcoholics, or drug addicts, or people who really do need to lose weight, these anorexics can be motivated only by themselves. It has to come from within. They can't be lectured, scolded, scared, threatened, or anything else. It may work for the short haul, but not for the long haul. They have to be treated professionally and have their walls broken down. Once they see themselves for what they are and their situation for what it is, then they can decide to do something about it or not."

"What does God have to do with that?"

"Well—and again, this is my opinion—her deepest need is to know where she stands in the universe. I mean, don't you think if she knew God cared about her, it would make a big difference in how she felt about herself? Self image is what this is all about. Did you hear her saying she was fat? And did you see who she was saying that to?"

"A nurse?"

"A fat nurse! Someone twice her size! It's ridiculous. She's truly ill, and she doesn't even know it."

"What can I do for her?"

"Professionally I know that anyone who can offer her care and counsel has the best chance. Personally, I think only someone who can get her in contact with God has a real chance."

"Well, I'm a Christian, so maybe I can help," I said.

She smiled and gave me a bear hug. "Am I glad to hear that!" she said. "Am I ever glad to hear that! Visit me next week, and let's plan strategy."

10

The Finals

I could tell Nurse Betty Bolla about Traci, but I couldn't tell Mr. and Mrs. Kent. Maybe I should have, but they were still embarrassed over what Andy had done to me with Jimmy's horse and all that. Plus I figured that the nurse was right. Traci would have to wake up to this problem herself. Anyway, from what I heard from Andy and Traci, it seemed her parents might have been part of the problem.

Everything seemed to fall into place for me and mean more than it had when I first heard or saw it. I remembered how she was so worried about her grades, even though they were all A's. She couldn't stand to see Andy under pressure in any situation where he might not succeed. She was worried about having got me in trouble with my mother because I was outside talking when she got home. And then she felt she knew what her parents thought about her by what they said about her friends.

No wonder she felt she needed something in her life she could control. One thing I knew for sure: I had no idea how to handle someone who had this kind of illness. I wondered if she would show up at our final game the next afternoon.

When I got there, Andy was already on the field. I jogged out to him. "Your sister coming today? Just wonderin'."

"Sure ya are."

"I am!"

"You're a little young for her, aren't you, Dallas?"

That irritated me. "Let's let her be the judge of that."

That surprised him. "There's your answer," he said, nodding toward the stands.

There she was, with her and Andy's parents. She wore bulky clothes, and I'm sure it was just my imagination, but she looked even smaller and thinner than the day before.

"By the way," Andy added, "it would mean a lot to my dad if you would let me lead off today."

"Lead off?"

"Or bat in the top half of the order somewhere. You know, because my dad's here."

"Everybody's dad is here today, Andy," I said. "Maybe I should let everybody lead off."

"C'mon, Dallas, just this once?"

I looked at him and shook my head. I couldn't believe what I was hearing. "This your idea?" I asked.

He shook his head and looked embarrassed. His father had put him up to this. "You're batting ninth and playing right, as usual," I said, "and if your dad asks if you talked to me about moving you, tell him yes. To put you above the team is not right, Andy, and you know it."

"I know."

"And maybe you can't tell your dad that, but I'm sure not going to cave in to him."

Beach had come back and beaten the favored Deerfield in the lower bracket semifinal, so we would face a very talented, very fast, well-coached, and disciplined team. The Beach Bearcats had won the league championship in their town and had been seeded third in our tournament. Both final teams had been a surprise; we had been seeded fourth.

Because of our ten-run rule victory Thursday night, I still had four innings I could pitch. Before the game we debated about whether I should start or finish.

"Cory and I each have two left," Bugsy said. "So let us start until we get in trouble, and then if we need you to go into extra innings, you'll be available."

I liked that idea and started Bugsy, with Cory to come in in the third. It started out great. Bugsy pitched two perfect innings, and Cory—though he allowed two hits and loaded the bases on a walk—pitched out of trouble in the bottom of the third. We went into the top of the fourth in a scoreless tie.

Ryan was on third with two out and Brent at the plate when we came the closest to scoring. Brent lifted a lazy pop fly out behind second that was too short for the center fielder and too far for the shortstop or second baseman—I thought. Ryan left with the pitch and crossed the plate long before the ball came down. We were cheering our first run when the second baseman took a mighty dive, slid along the grass, and snagged the ball.

In the bottom of the fourth, Cory ran into trouble. He walked the first two hitters, then hit the next with a pitch.

I trotted to the mound. "Gettin' tired?"

"No, let me keep tryin', Dal. I'm OK."

"It looks like you're struggling."

"Ask Jimmy. He'll tell ya I still got stuff on the ball."

"The ball's still movin', Dal," Jimmy said, "but I wouldn't let him walk or hit anyone else, and a big hit's gonna put us behind. Their guy has great control, and we're gonna have trouble scorin' off them."

I nodded. "Prove yourself with this hitter, Cor'. Otherwise, you and I are changin' places."

I have to hand it to him. Cory got the next three pitches over. The first was a strike off the outside corner on a left-handed hitter. The next caught the inside corner at the knee. I thought sure Cory would waste a pitch, but maybe he didn't want to risk a wild pitch that would score a run. He threw a

83

nice, slow, fat pitch on the outside corner at the letters, and Lefty teed off. The shot hit the left center-field fence on the fly, scoring all three runners. Only a fantastic throw by Ryan kept the big hitter at second.

I almost thought twice about putting Cory at second after the way he had battled that hitter, but he turned without waiting for me and tossed me the ball.

"Good try," I told him, as I approached the mound. There were no outs. I could still pitch up to four innings.

I badly wanted to keep that fourth run from scoring, but even though I pitched well, it wasn't to be. I got the first hitter to ground out to first, but the ball was hit slowly enough that the runner reached third. One out.

On a ground ball up the middle, one I was sure Bugsy could get to, I screamed, "Get two!" and Cory drifted over to second. Bugsy fielded the ball and flipped it to Cory, but Cory had trouble digging it out of his glove as he stepped on second. His throw to first was on the mark but late, and the run scored.

I struck out the next hitter, but we were down 4-0 going into the top of the second to last inning.

"We need a couple right now!" I said as we prepared to hit.

Jimmy led off by reaching on an error and taking second on a passed ball. I was afraid he would never get there. I asked Andy to bunt Jimmy to third, and he argued with me.

"What good is one run gonna do us? I make an out, and that's it."

"We need every run we can get, Andy, and you struck out against this guy, you know."

" 'Cause I'm hittin' ninth, that's why."

He was making his usual sense. None. "How 'bout you play and let me manage, OK?" I said.

He pursed his lips and shook his head, then proceeded to lay down a perfect bunt. In fact, he almost beat it out. Jimmy wound up on third with one out. I told Cory to try to hit something to the right side, giving Jimmy a chance to score. It was asking a lot, and I worried about sacrificing yet another out for the sake of one run, but we had to get on the board.

Cory has the best bat control on our team, and he drove a grounder to second. Jimmy had picked up the hit-and-run sign, so he took off for the plate. He's so slow, and the second baseman was so good, I was afraid we'd blown it. But the throw was high, and Jimmy was barreling pretty well, so he was safe, and Cory reached first.

Cory stole second, then tagged up and moved to third on a fly to center by Bugsy. The throw to third was in the dirt and skipped past the pitcher, who was backing up the play. Cory streaked home with our second run.

I wished someone were on base when I came up with two outs, but no one was, so I decided to go for a homer. I should never do that. I reached and swung too hard and popped out to the first baseman.

We got Beach out three up and three down in the bottom of the fifth and came in for our last chance. It was up to Toby, Jack, and Ryan.

Toby led off with a smash between the right and center fielders but made the huge mistake of trying to stretch a double into a triple and getting tagged out. First he ignored my stop sign from the coaching box at third, and then he slid, but too late. It was wrong and it was foolish, given the score and the inning. But we're a team first and individuals second, and I was real proud of the guys who slapped him on the back and told him it was a good effort.

"It was not!" he shouted, almost crying. "It was stupid, and if we lose it's my fault!"

"Just learn from it, Tob'," I said. "You've played a great game. Let's stay in it."

Jack hit a screamer down the third base line that went all the way to the fence. I gave him a frantic stop sign as he rounded second, and he skidded and dove back in. The one thing Jack has never caught on to, being a good athlete but being retarded, is the finer points of running the bases.

I called time and ran out to him.

"Jack, would you mind if I replaced you with Kyle to run for you?"

"I'm fast!"

"I know. You're faster than Kyle, but I'd rather have Kyle in here right now. Is that all right?"

"If that's what you want."

"Pinch runner!" I told the ump, and Jack traded places with Kyle on the bench.

"Kyle," I said, "let's not try to steal. Your run is meaningless unless we can get another, so do what you have to do."

He knew exactly what I meant, and he did the right thing. When Ryan hit a grounder to short, the shortstop checked Kyle back to second, but Kyle fell down on purpose on his way back, leaving himself enough room to grab the bag when he needed to.

The shortstop hesitated, then dove at him, and Kyle was back in safely, with Ryan at first and only one out. The tying runs were on.

I called for a double steal, hoping to eliminate the force and also hoping they might mistakenly walk Brent to get to Jimmy. Their catcher did not throw, so now we had runners on second and third, one out, and Brent up.

Brent lifted a high, deep fly to right field. I hollered for Kyle and Ryan to tag up. The right fielder caught the ball just in front of the fence and heaved the ball toward the plate. Kyle was off like a shot with the catch and scored easily. Ryan, at second, headed for third but couldn't avoid a peek at the plate to be sure Kyle had scored.

He raised a fist as he saw Kyle cross the plate, and he missed my slide sign. The first baseman, serving as the cutoff man on the play, caught the throw near the mound and fired to third. Ryan was tagged out on a strange, run-producing double play that suddenly, stunningly, ended the game.

It was as if we had been punched in the stomach. Ryan buried his face in his hands and cried. The rest of the team gathered around to encourage him and to congratulate the winners. It was a bitter loss, but I was glad we had learned some lessons about sportsmanship and teamwork.

I looked up in time to see Mr. Kent wave disgustedly at the field and leave with his wife, not even waiting for Andy. My parents came down from the stands and hugged me, and I saw Traci watching from the backstop.

I ran to her. "I'm still going to that softball game on the other diamond," I said. "You coming?"

"Aren't your parents upset with you?"

"Why would they be upset with me?"

"You lost, didn't you?"

"We got beat. I did my best. How could they be mad about that?"

She shook her head slowly. "Yeah, let's go watch some softball."

11

The Referral

Our meeting in the stands at the pee-wee softball tournament in Park City was just the first of many conversations we had over the next several weeks. When her name was not listed with the others who had made the varsity cheerleading squad that Monday, and her friend Jill had been named captain, I saw Traci Kent nearly fade away.

At the softball game she had marveled at the relationship I seemed to have with my parents, and she asked a lot of questions about how I got along with my little sisters. She had watched, she said, how I was with the players on the Baker Street Sports Club baseball team.

"Doesn't it drive you crazy if they do better than you, or if you make an error or an out in a crucial situation?"

"Sometimes it does, but it doesn't help me to worry about it. I can only do the best I can do. Who can ask for more than that?"

Traci denied starving herself, but no one could get her to eat much. Her father hollered at her, and her mother pleaded with her. Andy told her she looked terrible. Just as the nurse said, Traci's weight dropped until her face was long and drawn, her hair lost its luster, and her clothes hung on her like blankets.

Her grades fell too, and she went from being on the high honor roll three of four quarters as a freshman to being on academic probation. Nearly every day I checked with her, and about once a week I visited the nurse at her high school. We prayed together for Traci, but Miss Bolla reminded me over and over that "there's little anyone can do for her until she makes up her mind that she needs help."

I invited Traci to church, but she wouldn't come. I told her God loved her and cared about her, but it was as if she didn't hear me.

"I don't want to go anywhere in public until I trim down some."

. I quit arguing with her about her weight. I couldn't imagine that she didn't know she had lost several pounds. How much did she want to lose?

"You go to school everyday," I said.

"I have no choice. If I had a choice, I wouldn't go. I'm so depressed."

"You're depressed because you're not well," I said.

"Not well?" she said. "I've never felt better."

One Friday night, just after midnight, I heard something hit my bedroom window. I thought it was a twig that had blown off a tree, but it woke me enough that I heard it clearly the second time. It was a pebble. A few seconds later, another one hit, and I scrambled to the window and peered out. There, under the utility light in our gravel driveway, stood Andy Kent motioning for me to come down.

I slipped down there quietly without waking the family, not because I was doing anything wrong but because I didn't want to disturb them.

Andy was crying. "You've got to do something for Traci," he sobbed.

"What's wrong?"

"You know what's wrong. The same thing that's been wrong for weeks!"

"But what happened?"

"I don't want to talk about it."

"C'mere," I said and walked toward the shed. I sat with my back against the wall under the shed light.

Andy sat beside me and cried some more.

"Listen," I said, "I need to know what happened or I can't help.

"I caught her," he said suddenly.

"Caught her doing what?"

"Stuffing herself."

"Well, that's good! She hasn't been eating. She needs to eat."

"Dallas! You didn't see her! She looked like a maniac. She was out of control. She had dragged a bunch of boxes down onto the basement steps. I heard some noise and found her there. Her hair was a mess. I opened the door, and she didn't even see me. She sat with her back to me, jamming her hands down inside boxes of cereal and crackers. Her cheeks bulged with food, and she was gasping for breath, hardly chewing, trying to swallow, coughing. It was terrible."

"Wow," I said. "Did she ever know you were there?"

"Yes. I said, 'Traci,' and she froze without turning around. She chewed and swallowed what she had in her mouth, then turned slowly and tried to smile at me. Her eyes looked wild, she was still breathing hard. 'I was just getting a snack,' she said. 'Want any?' All I could do was shake my head and move back up the stairs. She made a big show about calmly carrying the boxes back up the stairs and putting them away. I didn't want to look like I was was spying on her, so I went back upstairs and got dressed. I knew I had to talk to you, so I snuck out."

"Well, I'm glad you did, but I don't know what I—"

He interrupted me. "That's not all, Dallas," he said. "When I went outside, the kitchen light was still on, so I peeked in the window. She was standing at the counter stuff-

91

ing herself again, only it wasn't crackers and cereal this time. It was pasta."

"Pasta?"

"Hard, dry, uncooked macaroni noodles."

"Gross!"

"Gross is right! I couldn't believe it. I didn't want to tell Mom and Dad, but I had to tell someone, and that's why I'm here."

I hardly knew what to say or do. "Do me a favor," I said. "I think Traci's going to be all right for tonight, and if I go talk to her, we're going to have to involve my parents and your parents. Why don't you go back home, and if she's still awake, tell her exactly what you saw and what you did."

"You mean seeing her stuffing herself and coming to tell you?"

"Yes."

"She'll kill me."

"No, she won't. She might get mad and scream and holler at you a little, but I'll bet she'll be impressed down deep that you care that much about her. Anyway, tell her you want her to talk to me and that I'll meet her anywhere she wants."

"I don't think this is gonna work."

"You got a better idea?"

He shook his head. "I'll try it."

"Call me early."

"Don't worry. Thanks, Dallas."

He rode off on his bike, and I didn't sleep much. Early in the morning I looked up Miss Bolla's phone number and called her at home. I apologized for bothering her and told her what was going on.

"This could be encouraging," she said. "I know that sounds strange, but these binges are the body's way of rebelling against starvation, and often they wake up the anorexic and prove to her that she's desperately in need of help. If she'll talk to you, you want to keep hammering home that point.

She's sick, she needs help, and she needs it now. But it's her decision."

"I don't know what to say to her, besides that. I mean, I'm not the person she needs help from."

"I'd be thrilled if she would seek my counsel, Dallas, but I have learned not to force myself on people. It doesn't work that way. I have a network of doctors and health care specialists I can call on, and I can counsel her myself. But it must be her choice. I can't emphasize that enough. I'll be here all day if you need to talk to me. I'll pray for you today. I hope she'll see you."

I was too nervous to eat breakfast, waiting for the call from Andy. That gave me time to decide on a little strategy. I wanted to point Traci toward making her own decisions about this, so when Andy called and said she had agreed to talk with me, I told him to tell her that I didn't believe it.

"What're you talkin' about, O'Neil? You said you'd see her, and now you're backin' out?"

"I'm not backing out."

"You know she was talkin' about killin' herself this morning? She said she wrote a note during the night but couldn't work up enough courage to go through with it."

I knew that when people start talking about killing themselves, they mean it. I didn't want to say or do anything that would push her to that, but Nurse Bolla's advice rang in my ears. "Tell her I won't believe her unless she tells me herself."

"O'Neil, you're crazy! What if she kills herself because of that?"

"Stay with her. Make sure she doesn't. If she starts talking that way, call me. But first tell her that she has to call me herself because I don't believe her."

"OK, but I think you're nuts."

In just a few minutes, the phone rang.

"I'll get it!" I shouted. "O'Neil residence. This is Dallas."

"Where?" came the weak voice of Traci Kent.

"Anywhere you say."

"The parking lot of the grocery store?"

"Olive Street?"

"Right. When, Dallas?"

"I'm on my way."

She hung up without another word.

I rode as fast as I could, remembering that I had not had breakfast yet and that we would have at least that in common. I also thought about the fact that I had pushed her into one decision already that morning. She had a location in mind, and I hadn't had to drag it out of her or talk her into it.

She had a shorter distance to ride than I did, yet I got there first. I sat on a car stop, watching the frontage road and Olive Street, and soon there she came, walking her bike. She looked so small and thin and weak, and walked so slowly that I wondered if she would make it. I wanted to run and help her, but I had the feeling she needed this to help show her how much she had weakened.

She saw me from a distance but didn't even wave. She simply trudged across the mostly empty parking lot and let her bike fall. She slowly sat next to me on the car stop, then stood, took off her sweater, and bundled it under her. I figured she had lost her natural padding. Her arms and legs looked like skin and bone.

"I'm in trouble, Dallas," she said, her voice a whisper.

"What's wrong?" I said.

"I still feel fat," she said, and I was about to throw my hands up in defeat. But she had said she felt fat, not that she was fat, like before.

"You do?"

She nodded. "But I'm not, am I?"

"No, you're not. How much do you weigh?"

"Do I have to tell you?"

I nodded.

"Eighty something."

94

"Fully clothed, and the something means eighty-even or eighty-one, am I right?"

"Eighty-two. What's wrong with me, Dallas?"

"You tell me."

"I'm out of control, and I have no one to talk to, no one to go to. You tell me to go to God, but I don't know how. You're the only person I can talk to, and you're twelve years old."

What could I say? That had been bothering me since the first time Andy had told her to talk to me. I was flattered that he thought I had something to offer, and she always said I was easy to talk to, but now I was in way over my head. I had no idea what to say.

"I need somebody older, Dallas. There's something really wrong with me. I think I'm going crazy. I starve myself and then I gorge myself, and then I feel so bad I want to kill myself. I think of nothing else twenty-four hours a day. I can't sleep. I can't concentrate. I need someone to talk to who understands this, who can help me."

"You've got the wrong person," I said sadly, not trying to be mean but just honest.

"I know," she said. "And it's unfair of me to dump it all on you."

"I don't mind," I said. "I just agree. You need a woman who knows all about this, one who can also lead you to God and to the professionals who can help you."

She buried her head in her hands and cried. "That sounds too good to be true," she said.

"I know just the person," I said.

She looked up at me with bloodshot eyes, then lowered her head again as if she didn't even have the strength to ask who I was talking about.

"Nurse Bolla from your school."

From somewhere I heard her muffled reply. "I've lied to her."

"She knows."

"She would bawl me out."

95

"No, she wouldn't." I said that with confidence because I knew better.

She breathed a huge sigh and lifted her head again. Her voice was quavery. She held out her hands. "Whatever," she said. "I can't go on like this. I'm ready for anything."

"Really? Anything? Even counseling that would include your parents?"

She thought about that one. She nodded slowly. "Anything."

"I could call her," I said, "but I won't speak for you."

She looked at me gravely. "I'll talk to her," she said.

I parked her bike at the rack next to mine, then had her follow me to a pay phone. I dug the number out of my pocket and dialed.

"Miss Bolla?" I said.

"Yes, Dallas, what is it?"

"I have someone here who wants to talk to you."

A NOTE TO THE READER

This book was selected by the same editors who prepare *Guideposts*, a monthly magazine filled with true stories of people's adventures in faith.

If you have found inspiration in this book, we think you'll find monthly help and inspiration in the exciting stories that appear in our magazine.

Guideposts is not sold on the newsstand. It's available by subscription only. And subscribing is easy. All you have to do is write Guideposts Associates, Inc., 39 Seminary Hill Road, Carmel, New York 10512. For those with special reading needs, *Guideposts* is published in Big Print, Braille, and Talking Magazine.

When you subscribe, each month you can count on receiving exciting new evidence of God's presence and His abiding love for His people.